St. James Infirmary

(Stories)

Steven Meloan

ROADSIDE PRESS

St. James Infirmary
Copyright ©Steven Meloan 2023
ISBN: 979-8-9861093-7-4

Editor: Michele McDannold

Roadside Press
Meredosia, IL

Foreword

During the last live performance of Jim Morrison's life (in New Orleans on December 12, 1970) he insisted on bellowing the jazz standard "St. James Infirmary" between the agreed songs on the set list. At the end of the show, he violently bored a hole in the stage by pounding the mic stand into the ground. Like that performance, and like the lyrics of "St. James Infirmary" itself, the stories in this volume are tinged with a devil-may-care rock and roll attitude as well as a few pangs of regret.

Here in the digital age it is easy to live vicariously through others, but Steven Meloan (and his brother Michael, a character in the text) went out to see life for themselves. From tales of crossing the Mojave Desert as small boys while moving to L.A. in the early 60s, to busking as street musicians in the shadow of the Berlin Wall in the 80s, Steven's stories are not so much about rock, but more infused with a rock sensibility within everyday life. From fiery domestic squabbles, to the Smell-O-Vision fad of the 60s, to sneaking underage drinks, to fleeting chances at love, to singing in the subways of Paris, Meloan has lived to tell about his adventures with grit, humor, and honesty. He describes an all night diner: "The unearthly brightness and neon trim felt like a space station." Or his first memory of Los Angeles: "....the distant roar of traffic, which I imagined to be the ocean."

In the same spirit that Henry Miller brought the voice of American bohemia to print, and Bukowski brought the voice of the blue-collar worker forth, Meloan is part of a movement of writers working to bring the voice of the garage rocker, the heads of the underground, and other cultural outsiders into literature. The effect of his lean poetic prose is raw, at times explosive, but often subtle in a way that is simply, cool.

In this world you have to go out and learn about life for yourself. Otherwise you might as well drown in academia, spend your life regurgitating quotes, or be fed ideas like baby birds by the last scavenger who arrived too late. As other people burrow further down the digital portal of memes and fluff that repeat like meaningless fractals, instead grab yourself a copy of this book, and let it be your companion on your next train ride, layover, road trip, or trip into yourself…and good luck.

—Westley Heine, Author of *Busking Blues: Recollections of a Chicago Street Musician & Squatter* and *12 Chicago Cabbies*.

Introduction

A few years back, I attended a San Francisco Lit gathering with my Sonoma writer-friend, Lisa Summers. We heard many inspired readings and performances. But during one of them, Lisa leaned over and whispered—"You know, there are plenty of great writers in Sonoma. We could put on a local version of this."

And so she did. Unlike so many offhand comments or great ideas, she actually made it happen.

Beginning in 2014, Lisa and Daedalus Howell, a North Bay writer and filmmaker, assembled quarterly events with their Sonoma Writers' Workshop group, held at the Bump Wine Cellars tasting room off the Sonoma Plaza. The inaugural night's theme was "Naked and Drunk"—the lineup including Daedalus Howell, AJ Petersen, Jonah Raskin, Lisa Summers, Stacey Tuel, and several open mic readers.

It was a gathering worthy of a wine-fueled Kerouac era North Beach event. During a particularly frenzied Beat-style reading by Jonah Raskin—a wildman writer and former Sonoma State Prof.—he first stripped off his tee shirt, then his pants...and finally his briefs. Mindful of the night's theme, he laid bare the words, and the skin.

"Don't ever do that again," Lisa told him afterward. But it was a memorable night!

A year or so later, I found my way into the fold, along with Carol Allison, and a rotating assortment of drop-in writers. With Steve Shane and Steve Della Maggiora on upright bass and accordion—providing coffeehouse-style musical backing—the cast was complete.

It's often said that necessity is the mother of invention. The Bump gatherings have been an essential catalyst for these stories. After several years of such readings, I one day recognized that I'd amassed a fairly sizable collection. A shout-out as well to Deb Carlen, editor of the Sonoma Valley Sun's Creative Arts section, which first published several of these pieces. And also to Evan Karp and his wonderful Quiet Lightning literary events in San Francisco, where another piece here was first read.

Special thanks additionally to Sarah Ford and Lisa Summers, for stellar copyediting. And to Mieko and Geordie of Bump Cellars, for seasonally surrendering their wonderful tasting room space to a circus of literary crazies. And finally, a tip of the hat to my boyhood friend Robert Rico, who in the 1980s sent me a letter that said—"I love the postcards you send from San Francisco, such great stories and descriptions. You should consider writing."

...And so I did.

Contents

Dedicated to all those along the way...for who they were, who they are, and who they may be. And with particular thanks to Margaret L. White and Veronica Scott, without whom the road might have been very different.

"Lights flicker from the opposite loft
In this room the heat pipes just cough
The country music station plays soft
But there's nothing, really nothing to turn off
Just Louise and her lover so entwined
And these visions of Johanna that conquer my mind"

"Visions of Johanna"
Bob Dylan

Googies

It had been a long, hard cross-country drive west, in our boat-like 1960s Mercury cruiser. My parents could only cover a few hundred miles a day—because my brother and I were always hungry, or bored, or needed to pee. After a half-day of driving, my father would finally give in, check us into a roadside Motor Hotel, where we would swim, eat burgers, bounce like monkeys between beds in the musty room, and then fall into exhausted sleep.

The final stretch had seemed an eternity of highway—parched plains, tin-badge sheriffs wanting payments for (we suspected) manufactured infractions…and then the haunted moonlit expanse of the Mojave Desert. My parents had purchased an after-factory A/C for our new car—a rare luxury for the time. But because of it, the car was endlessly overheating.

Knowing nothing about such things, my college-professor father opened the hood, cars roaring past us in the starry night. He pulled out his handkerchief, loosening the radiator cap, unleashing a boiling geyser of water that blew ten feet into the air. He howled into the night like a wounded animal. My mother applied Vicks VapoRub (there in case my brother or I fell ill) to his badly blistered forearm, and we continued on into the desert expanse.

So after all that, it was a relief to have finally arrived—to be in Los Angeles. We pulled in at midnight off the Harbor Freeway, our legs stiff, our butts numb. Rolling down the windows brought the distant roar of traffic, which I imagined to be the ocean. The breeze carried with it the smell of oranges and dust, and other new and indefinable things.

And Downtown L.A. wasn't much back then, almost a ghost town by night. My brother whispered over to me, "…It's not very nice here, is it? Not like Indiana."

My mother peered out into the solitary darkness, involuntarily gathering her coat around her. I watched her tired face lit in pale fluorescence, reflected in the car's window glass.

And once again, my brother and I needed a snack, and had to pee. A diner at the corner of Pershing Square glowed in the distance like a solitary oasis—neon-red and fluorescent-white splashing out onto the dark oily streets. "Googies"—the two O's of the sign forming curious cartoon eyes.

Cruising past, we saw solitary men inside hunched on red naugahyde stools, nursing cups of coffee, and maybe a slice of pie. I wondered what people were doing out at that hour, and all alone.

"I'm not taking the children in there," my mother said as we pulled up to the curb. "It's full of bums!"

My father, tired from the road and his arm still raw, growled back—"If they get hungry enough, they'll get used to it!"

We were the only family in the place, the young waitress giving us a booth by the window. The unearthly brightness and neon trim felt like a space station. At a nearby stool, a man nervously traced a finger along the pastel shapes etched in the countertop, stubbing out the last of a cigarette, and then lighting another.

But after a fountain Coke, a grilled cheese, and fries, all felt right again with the world. Even my father seemed in better spirits. We checked into our hotel—the "Cloud Motel," just west of downtown. The rooms smelled of stale cigarettes and bleach. But a glowing swimming pool hummed in the center courtyard, its lattice of turquoise light dancing in invitation.

The next morning, we all went sightseeing—billowing L.A. clouds against a painfully blue sky, impossibly tall palms swaying in the breeze, and the jacaranda trees in full purple bloom. It was before the era of smog, and the downtown gleamed like Oz.

When we came back to our room later that afternoon, though, we found my mother's dresses and blouses inexplicably stuffed into a plastic trash can in the hall outside the door. My father's face tightened in rage. Like a detective, he slowly unlocked the door of our room. Inside, three men in their underwear sat at a small round table, smoking cigars and playing cards. Their wiry black chest hair spilled out from white-ribbed undershirts, and a lone woman lounged on a far chair, her legs crossed, wearing nothing but a bra and panties.

"What the *hell* are you doing in my room!" my father snarled.

"What the hell are you doing in my room?" a man who appeared to be the leader of the group shot back.

My father spun out to the hall, grabbed the trash can filled with my mother's clothes, emptied the contents into the trunk of our Mercury, and then headed for the hotel office. My brother and I stood outside with my mother, her arms wrapped around us. Inside the glass enclosure, we saw my father waving his arms, his mouth contorting into vague obscenities. In response to something the desk clerk said, my father drop-kicked the plastic trash can clear across the office lobby. He'd never been good at sports, but it was an impressive shot.

Minutes later, he emerged with a new room key. "There's a convention nearby," he said, his face still red, "and they needed the larger rooms. It's apparently how they do things here. But we're getting the new room for free—and for the rest of the week."

I looked at my parents as we made our way to the new room, trying to decide from their expressions whether this turn of events was a good thing, or a bad thing. My father suggested we all put on our suits and go for a swim.

"...Welcome to L.A.," he said.

Hold Me Tighter

It was the kind of place…where it seemed like almost anything could happen. Sweetwater was a local dive bar and club, just across the sand from the Redondo Beach pier—frayed and braided nautical rope spiraling up the inside support beams, tables and chairs that had seen way better days, and a bleached and feathered animal skull mounted high above the stage, like something out of an early Eagles album.

My first night there, a full-blown barroom brawl erupted. The country band was halfway through "Ladies Love Outlaws," when someone in the packed house apparently decided to test the theory. Fists and bodies were soon flying, tables overturned, and chairs thrown. And through it all, the band kept playing, the sweating masses throbbing to the raw, country beat—"… *And outlaws touch ladies, somewhere deep down in their soul."* My brother and I edged along the back wall as the maelstrom expanded, fists arcing just inches from our faces, until we finally made it out to the cool night air.

I later started playing Open Mic nights there, bringing a group of guy friends along—who mainly came for the girls and the beer. I never really smoked much, but for some reason I did on those nights. It just seemed the thing to do, like in an after-sex movie scene. As I lit up after my set one night, the girl to my right tapped me on the shoulder, asked if I had an extra. I offered her one, and lit it for her. She was a beach girl—low-cut tube top, and faded jeans with stylishly placed tears. She took a hungry drag on the smoke, eying me. "Natalie," she said, shaking hands.

The headlining band was good—originals that were a cross between Elvis Costello and Leonard Cohen. Between songs we got to talking more, and then I felt Natalie's side-glances on me from time to time.

The band soon said that they were taking a break, but would be "right back." Just then, Natalie's girlfriend started gathering up her stuff, and the two of them began talking. A moment later, she touched me on the shoulder. "Hey, I really like this band, but my girlfriend has to head out, to be up early for work. Do you think you could give me a ride if I stayed?" I nodded, said it was not a problem.

We went through several more beers, and most of the next set. "...I should probably hit it," she said finally, eyeing me. In the movies, when the guy meets the girl on a night out, and they somehow end up leaving together, the guy-buddies always watch as they go. And that happened. Smith winked and gave me a thumbs-up as she and I headed to the door.

Somehow, it never even seemed a question that I would come in—it just felt like a given. But as we were about to enter her apartment, Natalie suddenly held a conspiratorial finger to her lips. "You need to hide out while I pay the babysitter," she whispered. My eyes widened. With no further explanation, she accordioned the hall closet door, and nudged me inside.

Surrounded by jackets and sweaters in the dark space, I looked out through the wooden slats onto the dimly lit hall. I heard Natalie trading verbal notes with what sounded like a teenage girl. She thanked her finally—and I wondered in a panic whether the girl might have a jacket hanging in the closet. But then I heard the front door close.

I expected to soon be rescued, but then Natalie and a young boy began talking down the hall. "No…not tonight, sweetie, it's already *way* past your bedtime," she said. "I'll read you a story tomorrow night…I promise!"

More minutes passed. I was beginning to think she'd forgotten me, or was perhaps insane. But then the door finally accordioned back open. "The coast is clear," she grinned.

It was a nice apartment—sofa combo, stereo system, prints of Europe on the walls, with a stunning image of the stairs at Sacré-Coeur by moonlight. She got beers from the fridge, and we sat across from one another on the sofa—doing the dance, seeing where things might lead. I slugged back some of the beer, and we talked, her eyes penetrating, almost searching. She put Warren Zevon on the turntable—rising and mournful classical guitar strains, a tale of doomed love. *"I hear mariachi static on the radio, and the tubes they glow in the dark. … Carmelita, hold me tighter, I think I'm sinking down."*

I took another pull of the beer, and checked out the album cover—Zevon in a dinner jacket, suave, side-lit, bathed in blue. His hair was perfect. The tortured tale and the swirl of the music pulled me in, and I began reading along to the lyrics. But then as the song faded, I looked up, and realized that Natalie was fast asleep. Unsure what to do at first, I finally crept over and lifted the needle from the record. Glancing back, Natalie's head rested awkwardly on the couch's side arm. She began to quietly snore.

I wondered whether I should wake her. I finally took a folded blanket from the end of the couch, and gently covered her. Then I went to check on the boy. The door was open, and he was also sound asleep. I turned on the bathroom light, so he wouldn't be afraid. Then I crept out, locking the door behind me.

Stepping into the late-night air, it felt like some strange dream. Some say that the heart wants what it wants. And I guess that's true. She'd taken a total stranger into her home, and then passed out, leaving her young son asleep in the other room.

When we'd first started talking that night, Natalie had jotted down her number. The next day, I found it crumpled in my pocket. I called and left a message, said I was glad we'd met, and that we should get together again. But I never heard back.

A few days later, I played again at the Sweetwater Open Mic. I wondered whether she might be there. Over beers, the guys couldn't wait to hear what had happened. And I told them.

"Oh, man!" Smith guffawed. "You drop the sweetest little thing in this guy's lap, and he *still* blows it!" He elbowed the others. "He couldn't get it up, right…right!" They all laughed, slapping their thighs. I smiled back, agreeing that was what had happened.

And then it came my turn to play. In the movies, when things don't work out, when all hope seems lost, the girl suddenly reappears—at the perfect magical moment. And there, in the blue stage light, I looked out, hoping to somehow see Natalie through the smoky haze.

I paused, closed my eyes, and strummed the sad opening strains of "Carmelita."

Smell-O-Vision

It was the early 1960s , and "Smell-O-Vision" made its debut at our local theater. Coming on the tail of the 3D movie craze, it was an in-theater system that released pre-programmed odors during key scenes of a movie—so the viewer could literally smell the story.

Gun barrel-sized metal tubes were mounted at the back of each theater seat, with a small hole at the tip. At pivotal moments in the film, the barrel in front of you would softly hiss, emitting an aroma for that particular scene: a bouquet of roses, a cigarette, a woman's perfume, a sizzling steak, or gun smoke after a wild shootout. We'd read in the paper that audiences would soon come to anticipate each new aroma as the story unfolded, with whispered amazement at the realism and immersion of the new medium.

I went with my parents on opening night. Because we were running late, we hadn't had time for dinner. My father said that we could all grab something afterward, but I told him I couldn't wait. So he bought me a warmed-over hot dog and chili fries from the theater snack counter. I wolfed it down in the neon-trimmed lobby, and then we made our way into the packed house…ready to go.

But it soon became apparent that things weren't sitting well. My intestines began to churn, like there was something alive in there. It was all I could do to hold things in. I was getting increasingly desperate, but there was finally a particularly noisy scene in the film—with clattering city traffic and honking car horns. Sensing my opportunity, I leaned up to one side, slowly letting it out. I figured that if anyone heard, they might just think it had been the Smell-O-Vision barrel in front of them.

Mission accomplished.

But just then, the movie cut to an indoor hotel scene, with a group of unkempt, gangster-looking men in undershirts, drinking, scratching their hairy chests, plotting a revenge hit. What I'd just done slowly wafted out into the theater. People nearby began shifting in their seats, heatedly whispering to one another.

"Oh, *man!*" I heard someone exclaim.

Expressions of disbelief soon turned to revulsion and horror. A woman nearby held a lace handkerchief up to her face. "Well, I never!" she said to her husband.

"Really…they're actually doing that?!" said another man. People began fanning their Smell-O-Vision brochures in front of their faces. I pinched myself, trying hard not to laugh.

When the film was over, I heard a man in the lobby complaining to the theater manager. "Smells like that…in a movie! Are you serious? That was *totally* uncool, man!"

"Was that you?" my father whispered as we headed out the lobby door, a look of fiendish delight on his face. I nodded sheepishly, and he discreetly high-fived me.

Smell-O-Vision only lasted a year or two afterward, soon dying an early death. But I've often wondered whether I helped bring it down.

The Swan

I told you about the swans, that they live in the park…

It was in the fifth month of her forty-second year. Ghosts would hover around the room. Theresa was busy unloading laundry from her car.

"…Why are you doin' laundry on a Saturday night?" a voice asked.

She turned. Over by the bus stop stood a man, hidden in the shadows. She briefly considered running.

"You look familiar," the man said. "Did you ever go to Berkeley?"

He emerged into a circle of light, a short, squat man in his fifties. "Hey, hey, who are the flowers for?" His speech was fast and clipped, but with a harmless touch of New York to it. Theresa began to soften.

"You sure ask a lot of questions for someone from Poughkeepsie," she quipped.

"Hey, I like that, a girl with some fire in her! OK, here's just one more, what's your number?"

"No, I don't think so," said Theresa. "I don't even know you."

"Fair enough! …I'm Al," he said, bowing grandly, "and you are…"

"Theresa," she answered hesitantly, but also slightly charmed.

Just then, the *1 California* bus hissed past, pulling to the curb. "Uh-oh, I have to go. Tell me, quick!" he said.

She hesitated, caught herself smiling, then said "Johnson, Theresa Johnson — it's in the book."

"Got it!" he rejoiced.

She watched him as the bus pulled away, lumbering down the aisle, almost unsteady on his feet. He dropped down heavily at a seat by the window.

Theresa shook her head, still smiling. "What have I done?" she said to herself.

Inside, she laid out her pantyhose on the painted brick hearth, like a sacrifice before the blue flame of the heater. The room was stiflingly warm. "Hi Monkey!" she said, to a stuffed figure on her bookshelf.

Monkey first came to her from her niece. Theresa knew he was alive. "Look at his eyes," she told friends, "they follow you!" She'd had to re-stuff him several times over the years, and didn't play with him as much as she'd like to anymore, for fear of wearing him out.

She flipped on the bedroom light and began folding the still-warm laundry. On the wall hung a print of a medieval painting — a young man, obviously a Prince, tenderly bending over a young woman, about to kiss her. In the girl's lap lay a garland of wildflowers. She wore a halo, and her skin shone like porcelain. The image had faded over the years, but it still brought Theresa great pleasure.

The next night, Al called. "Hey, hey, remember me?" he machine-gunned. She smiled wistfully, fighting off the desire to roll her eyes. As they talked, she wondered why the world was as it is, why he couldn't be the man she wished him to be.

But then he began discussing Baroque music. Theresa

suddenly became more attentive — she'd been a composition major in school.

"I'm lookin' for somebody to collaborate wit'," he said. "Someone who knows Basso Contin'uo." It sounded so comical, hearing theory spoken in a Bronx accent. Al explained that he was a physicist, and that he was exploring the effects of music, particularly of the Baroque style, on the nervous system. He needed a composer to aid in his experiments. He thought that she might be the one, that their having met might be fate. Theresa grew increasingly intrigued. She quizzed him on several theory points. He passed with flying colors.

She asked him how he had gotten into physics. "You don't seem like my impression of a scientist," she said.

"Ah, that's because I'm not!" Al replied.

He told her how he had once been a foreign ambassador to Indonesia. He'd been seriously injured after falling out of the back of a pick-up truck, sustaining a subdural hematoma. As a result of the injury, he'd lapsed into a year-long coma. When he finally came to, though, his IQ was found to have enormously increased. "It went way off the Richter scale!" he said. But, by his own admission, it also left him "kind of crazy."

It all sounded so farcical, she thought. Yet, the enthusiasm in his voice, the lilt when he spoke, slowly worked a kind of magic on her. There was a certain poetry to his words. She wanted to disbelieve him, but found that she could not.

Theresa suddenly wanted to freeze the moment, to stop him while she felt this way, before he might say something to ruin it. She interrupted, telling him that she had to go. "But I'm glad you called!" she said. "Call me again, OK?"

As she hung up, Theresa glanced across the room. Monkey was smiling at her.

That night she had a dream. *The Voices* spoke to her again. She was flying. There were fields of emerald green below. The sun reflected up from a chain of perfectly still lakes — flashing, as if from the surface of mirrors. It was hard to see where she was going, but then she realized that it no longer mattered. When she closed her eyes, she *knew* which way to go. Just then, a gentle voice said — "He will come to you..."

Theresa had agreed to meet Al at a Jewish deli in her neighborhood, and arrived early, checking her lipstick and hair in the bathroom mirror. He arrived late, and entered wearing an oily, blue windbreaker and loose fitting corduroy slacks. Up close, he looked like a cross between a homeless person and a disheveled college professor.

"Hey, hi!" he said, with a broad, child-like smile. As he sat down, he removed a knit, Sherlock Holmes-style cap. He wore enormous plastic sunglasses that gave him an otherworldly, fly-like quality. "Oops, almost forgot," he said, taking them off. "They're UV filters," he explained, "prevents cataracts. You should get some, they come in all colors."

He wasn't much to look at, she thought, but his green eyes were gentle and wise. There was something very sweet about him, in spite of everything. Beneath the table Al set down several plastic bags. One held a sheaf of well-worn papers. The other, ice cubes. He explained that the accident in Indonesia had left him thirsty all of the time. It was a mystery to the doctors. He'd found a place in Berkeley that made his brand, specially shaped, "like tiny sand dollars," he said. The increased surface area maximized the cooling effect, he explained.

"Oh, hey, hey! Let me show you this," he said, changing the subject. He rummaged through his bag of papers, extracting a tiny black box. It looked as if it might contain a ring. On top, in bold white letters, was inscribed "IBM." He opened it toward her, like a jeweler. Inside, resting on delicate prongs was an amber colored, gem-like object. Al explained that it was a super-conductor material that he had discovered and patented. He brought out diagrams and pictures, detailing its crystalline structure. He said that the rhomboidal configuration was key to its properties.

Theresa found herself staring into his eyes as he spoke. The color reminded her of the lakes in her dream.

Suddenly, Al glanced down at his watch. "Uh-oh, gotta go! I'm already late," he said. Without explanation, he began packing up his bags. She felt as if a rug, which she at first had not wanted, but was just becoming accustomed to, was now being rolled up and taken away.

"Well, it was fun…" she proffered.

"It was more than fun," he said. "It was everything I knew it would be. I feel like I could fly with my eyes closed around you." And with that, he was gone.

That night, Theresa dreamed of the Prince on her wall. The first time, many years before, he had bent down over her, admiring her hair, whispering to her that it was like spun gold. And when she awoke, it was! Before that, it had been a dull, ash-blond. Afterward, everyone complimented her, asking what she had done. She simply smiled.

The next night Al called, asking her out to dinner. But there were so many stipulations it was nearly impossible to accommodate his schedule. "No, no," he said, "can't make that, have to watch *60 Minutes* then. No, I have an early lecture the next day, that's too late. Uh-uh, I'm busy that night — has to be tonight. OK, yeah, 7:45 sounds perfect!" he finally agreed.

They ate in North Beach, at a small Italian bistro. But

the dinner proved forced and increasingly uncomfortable. Everything he said somehow grated on her. Theresa ordered a glass of wine, hoping to lose herself in it, and then get home early.

But after a while, Al seemed to loosen-up. He engaged the waitress, making her laugh with his jokes, winking at the punch lines. Theresa smiled over at him, wondering now if it had been her fault all along. In the flickering light of the table candle he looked quirky, but also somehow charming. He suddenly paused in their conversation, staring deeply into her eyes, admiring her "golden" hair.

Afterward, Al suggested dessert at his favorite café, raving about their banana-nut cake. Theresa let him out to order while she parked the car. But when she returned, he was standing out by the front door. "There's a problem," he said, "you'll have to order." Theresa asked him what had happened, but he simply looked down.

Inside, she ordered two pieces of the banana cake. The woman at the counter was alternately staring at her and over at Al. Theresa brought the enormous helpings back to their table by the window. "So, are you going to treat me to dessert?" she teased him.

"Nope, nope, not one penny for your body, not one penny!"

She jumped on him. "I can't believe you would say that. I drove all the way over to Berkeley to get you. I didn't say anything about dinner, but this is dessert. You asked ME out!"

"I would've paid, but they wouldn't serve me... It's a sign. Now I can't."

She was close to crying. "I'm sorry I ever met you!" she blurted out. Heads turned throughout the café.

"That's the trouble with you women," he said. "You're all masochists, you all want 'Mr. Right.' And you're sitting ducks for being taken advantage of, because of it."

Theresa felt she might hit him if she heard another word. Finally, she could no longer control herself. "How can you talk to me about wanting to be taken advantage of? What do you think you're doing?"

Al looked her in the eye. "With me, what you see is what you get," he said. "Have I ever misled you? No! I alone appreciate you for who you are. All of this," he said, sweeping the room with his hand, "is incidental. I KNOW who you are — I know about your hair. I've seen you flying. I'm the one in your dreams."

On the way back, they barely spoke. Al seemed to revert to his odd, earthly self. Theresa drove in silence, feeling that she had to get home, to sort through all that had happened.

Back in her apartment, she lit a candle and lay on the bed. The print on the wall shimmered in the yellow light, seeming to come to life. She finally closed her eyes, and slept more soundly than she had in years. In the morning, Theresa felt as if her entire body was glowing, vibrating. She was almost afraid to go out, for fear that others might see.

Al called the next day, enlisting her help in a "mission of mercy." He made no mention of the previous evening, or what had happened. In hushed tones he explained that there was a swan, named Gertrude, in the park near his home. Gertrude was the most intelligent swan that anyone had ever seen, he reported. She seemed almost human — eating out of people's hands, nuzzling their arms, and looking dolefully up into their faces. But she had recently been attacked by a pack of dogs and nearly killed. She seemed to lack a normal fear of other animals.

The park officials had decided, for her own safety, to move her to the local zoo.

Al told her that he was spearheading a petition drive to save Gertrude, to keep her in the park. "If they send her off to the zoo, it will kill her," he said. "I know her."

They made a date the next day to see a Tibet exhibit at the local museum in Berkeley. That way, Al could pick up his Gertrude flyers from the area copy store. Theresa was happy to do it. The swan story had so touched her, she now felt more deeply for him than ever.

But when she arrived, Al seemed more confused than usual. Theresa helped him load his ice bag in the back seat of her car, carefully adjusting his seat belt when he got it tangled. He complained about the heat in the car, that the ice chips were melting too quickly.

At her insistence, they picked up the flyers first. She wanted to be able to concentrate on just the two of them. As he got back in the car, Theresa noticed that he had neglected to shave his Adam's apple, which was flecked with gray stubble. Settling into the seat, he suddenly announced that one of his shoes had fallen apart, and that he had to get a new one before they could go to the exhibit.

The shoes were Chinese ballet slippers, embroidered in gold. Al directed her to the tiny shop where he had bought them. Theresa waited patiently outside while he argued with the owner — demanding two new pairs for his trouble, and then afterward, complaining to her at how cheaply everything was made these days, and how no one takes pride in what they do anymore.

When they finally arrived at the exhibit, Al suddenly balked. Theresa thought that it might be a matter of money. She offered to pay his way, but he still refused. "I've seen it. It's not any good," he said.

She blew-up at him. "Then, why did you ask me to see it with you?"

"I thought it might work out," he said, "but look what happened."

Fuming, she turned the car around, getting back on the freeway and taking him home. They didn't speak the entire way. Al sat next to her, examining his new slippers like a child.

As he got out, she again exploded. "Why are you doing this to me? You know what we have, what we could be — you said it yourself!"

He stared back blankly. Picking up his flyers, he said, "You know, that swan has been more loving and understanding to me than any woman ever has."

Theresa drove home, dazed, numb. Nearly a week went by, with no word from Al. She tried to move on from him, but found that she could not. And then to make matters worse, he began calling again, but to ask advice about other women. She went along with it for a time, wondering whether it might be some convoluted ploy to win her back. And what choice did she really have? Something about their connection felt fated. Monkey stared back at her from across the room, seeming to agree.

Al's new love was a 30-year-old French gymnast. He said that he'd met her in the local park — that he met all of his women there. "I'm like a whale, scooping-up plankton," he said.

Her name was Solange. Al began calling Theresa almost nightly, rambling on about the gymnast. Theresa listened dutifully, advising him where she could. She sensed that there was some deeper purpose to it, a purpose that she had not yet divined.

Finally, she decided to fight fire with fire. She placed an online singles ad, plotting to ask his help in screening the replies. But to her consternation, he readily agreed — directing her to read him the letters over the phone, some of them several times. In one case, he even had her email him the man's photograph. She had determined not to actually answer any of the ads, but Theresa played up one in particular, a good-looking lawyer from Marin. She read his letter more slowly, providing inflections, inserting dramatic pauses.

"Nope, nope, he's all wrong, I can tell already," Al said. "Stay away from WASPy ones, or the earthy emotional types." She wondered how he had arrived at this assessment of the man, but was pleased nonetheless by his reaction. It's working, she thought.

One night he called and, after a long and rambling monologue about the two of them, said--"I'm only doing all of this for your own good."

Her hair stood on end. Maybe he really is my soul mate, she thought, but was sent to guide me here on earth. We can never be together — he knows that — so he's trying to help me in the only way that he can. He has to drive me away, she concluded.

With this new revelation, Theresa determined that she *would* go out on dates with the men from her ad. But Al invariably picked the worst ones for her. The dates were disasters, the men boring and self-absorbed. Theresa often found herself drifting off during reluctant dinners out, thinking of Al, as the men yammered-on about sports, their cars, and their careers. Finally, in complete frustration, she called-up Bob, the lawyer from Marin that Al had earlier nixed. He proved nothing like what she had expected — loved art, and literature, and music. They even enjoyed the same movies and ethnic food.

Bob laughed at her quirky stories, probing Theresa about her dreams, and even her musical compositions. He seemed fascinated by everything about her. "You're the most unusual woman I've ever met," he said. Theresa soon spent long evenings on the phone with him, talking until late into the night. She almost felt like a girl again. It was as if she had been traveling through winding rapids, and had now passed into a calm, mirrored pool.

But invariably, Al would call while she was talking to Bob. He seemed to have almost a sixth sense about it. At first she was polite, promising to call him right back — and always dutifully doing so. But it became increasingly annoying. One night, anxious to get back to Bob, she snapped at him — "You're calling too much, give me room to breathe!"

"Don't flatter yourself," he said. "I'm not interested in you. I told you, I'm just trying to help you. Is this how you thank me?"

"I have to go," she said flatly.

Bob was everything she had ever wanted in a man. He even mentioned their living together.

Several nights later, Al called, sounding very upset. He finally admitted to Theresa that the gymnast, Solange, had left him. Theresa tried to console him, but in truth, she was drifting off, thinking about Bob. She finally got away by pretending that someone was at her front door. But Al continued calling — his neediness increasingly suffocating.

And then, they took Gertrude away. Al was in tears the night he called. "They can't do this, I won't let them!" he moaned. Theresa tried to reassure him, telling him that the battle was not lost, but he was inconsolable.

She went away with Bob that weekend. He again mentioned moving in together.

The messages from Al went on for weeks. At one point, he broke down and told Theresa how much he missed her — even more than Gertrude. She sighed to herself, looking down. Why wouldn't he set her free?

Finally, in the middle of a long and rambling Gertrude message on her machine one night, she picked up the call and shouted, "I caaaannn't!" The phone immediately clicked down at the other end.

And then the calls stopped.

Theresa began spending more and more time at Bob's. They walked through the woods, held hands beneath the stars, snuggled over late-night movies. Her life felt like a dream. Several weeks later, though, Bob became embroiled in an intense new legal case. He often came home late, exhausted and irritable. Soon, the case was all he could talk about—and with his job potentially on the line. He snapped at Theresa over dinner one night, saying that she needed to "come down to Earth," and that he was tired of hearing about her "stupid dreams." Finally, they both decided that they needed a break. She returned home.

That first night back, Theresa walked to the corner market to pick up groceries. Along the way, a front-page item in the weekly throwaway caught her attention. It read, "Swan Returned to Area Friends." She nearly cried.

Back home, she hurriedly set down her bags, dialing Al. But a recording said that the line had been disconnected, and with no forwarding number. The room lay still and dark — the cold sending a shiver through her. Monkey stared back quizzically.

Theresa ate dinner in a daze, going through the motions. In desperation she tried the number again, but got the same message. She lit a candle, and then lay on the bed. Through the window, a golden moon rose above the rooftops, full and large. She stared up at the print on the wall — as it shimmered in the candlelight. She closed her eyes and imagined him, in hopes that he might somehow call.

That night, Al appeared to her. It was him, yet somehow transformed — the Prince from her wall. "…They told me you would come," she whispered, her words sounding distant and strange, almost another's voice.

Silently he approached, gazing down upon her. She waited in anticipation, slowly parting her lips. From his long shining coat he produced a fiery jewel, the size of an eye, she thought. He placed it over her heart, and she felt hers flutter as he did. Then he brought it to her mouth, teasing her with it. He pressed it gently, caressing her lips — at first slightly burning, then slowly becoming the cool sensation of ice.

African Moon

The Peace Corps volunteers gathered at the outskirts of the small African village—first setting up their shortwave radio, and then staring up at the crescent moon. It was July 20, 1969.

The villagers were used to unusual activities on the part of their American guests, but this was something new. After watching them from afar for some time, they finally wandered out to the encampment.

"Is everything alright?" they asked.

"Everything is fine," smiled one of the Americans. "Amazing, in fact."

The lead villager scanned the assembled group—their small table with the battery-powered radio, water canteens, and various dried snacks. "Why do you listen to the radio," he asked, "and stare at the moon?"

"American astronauts have landed there," he answered, exultant. "And they will soon be walking on the surface!"

The man stared back at him, his expression doubtful. "How long does it take to get to the moon?" he asked, finally.

"Three days," one of the other volunteers proclaimed. "They just landed. We've been listening to their radio transmissions."

The villager furrowed his brow. "Three days? No, no," he said with grave certainty. "It take three days to get to Montubo...not to moon." The other villagers agreed, shaking their heads in disbelief.

The two groups stared back at one another.

"…That's right," said one of the Americans, finally. "You are correct, it does."

A lone fire flickered in the distance. Silver light painted the grasslands, seeming to go on forever, until finally melting into a vast field of stars.

The two groups stood side-by-side, listening to the small crackling radio—first staring at one another, and then up at a moon that now suddenly seemed brand new.

(Thanks to Doug Saxon for recounting his experiences of that day.)

Canyon Cottage

We reconnected over the Internet, after decades of distance. She was hard to find, but I put a certain amount of work into it— curiosity being what it is.

She'd been my college English Lit T.A. back then. I was on the six-year plan, and it had been my last semester, so we weren't really that far apart in age.

It had been an unusual class, in ways that I only later recognized—novel assignments about tortured relationships, men who were paralyzed, emotionally crippled, or who'd actually had their nuts blown off. One day in class, noting the difference between metaphor and simile, she'd cited a song lyric of the time as an example—"I had some dreams, they were clouds in my coffee," she said. But there was a genuine sadness in the delivery.

I'd visit her down in the subterranean T.A. office nooks, checking on assignments, or sharing bad poetry. But I think we both knew why I was there. She wore no bra, didn't shave her armpits, had a mysterious, knowing smile, and strangely seductive eyes. During one such visit, I'd attempted to describe her in some poetic and complementary way. She sat back, patiently listening to my overly long descriptive attempt, before finally correcting that hers were "bedroom eyes."

When the end of the semester came, I wasn't able to get the final paper in on time—some scheduling conflict on my end. But she was cool about it, left me a message at the English department with her home address, said that I could just drop it off. Even as clueless as I was back then, I knew that wasn't standard teacher/student protocol.

She lived in a little canyon cottage, along a narrow winding road nestled in the Hollywood Hills. You could almost imagine Joni Mitchell having once been there. I knocked on the wooden screen door, but no one was home. So I propped the envelope inside the screen, and left my number.

A few days later, there was a message on my machine—she'd gotten the paper, said if I was ever in the neighborhood again, to drop by. She left her number.

A week later, we'd arranged dinner. I showed up late—getting lost in the winding hills, even having been there before. It was nearly dark by the time I arrived, but she'd said to look for her Kansas plates at the curb. And that worked.

I guess she wasn't in Kansas anymore, and neither was I.

Looking back on it, she must have been waiting, and heard me arrive. She stood there in the doorway, framed in amber light, as I made my way through the rickety picket gate. Then she glanced back once, and I followed in.

We sat together on a creaking window seat overlooking a stunning canyon beyond, a sea of lights from similar cottages on the other side. She wound her finger through the red tie of an embroidered peasant blouse, staring out into the distance while I played with her cat Felicity, letting it bat at a long dried twig pulled from the yard.

The nearby restaurant where we ate had been her pick—set back from the street down a long, overgrown courtyard, with a bubbling tiled fountain at the center. And inside, intimate and candle lit, with hanging red lanterns, and waiters with slicked hair, wearing embroidered silk shirts.

I was a late bloomer, a cloistered science guy, and knew little about flirting, or dating small talk. But I remember her eyes in the candlelight.

I guess in the end, I cracked under the pressure—the older woman, and my teacher, even. And a dinner date right off the bat. Afterward, we came back to her place and listened to music—sitting together on an overstuffed old couch covered in a swirling paisley print. She put on Steely Dan's "Katy Lied"— the album cover picturing a giant, looming praying mantis.

"Katy tried, I was halfway crucified," the band crooned. Felicity rubbed against my leg, staring up at me with a penetrating gaze, as if she knew things that I did not.

We listened to more music, making small talk and drinking wine, waiting to see where things might go. It's hard to know sometimes why things don't happen, but they didn't. I finally made some halfway advances, but it came off as awkward, almost pathetic.

On the long drive home, I took it harder than I probably should have. Winding my little VW bug through the concrete corridors of the L.A. freeways, I began focusing on the sentinel-like abutments holding up the giant overpasses. Jimi Hendrix came on the radio—"*...Well I think I'm gonna tear myself up and, uh, go on down.*"

There in the jaundiced vapor lights of inner city L.A., still wounded and raw, I suddenly imagined swerving into one of the concrete pillars—thinking of the logistics, the outcome, and ultimately, the relief. It's hard to know how serious I really was, I can't quite say. But in the end, I didn't do it.

So that was it, I never saw her again. Strangely, I never called her, and she never called me.

And now here we were, decades later, catching up—both

married, kids on her side, kids on mine. She was back in Kansas. After several more email exchanges, I finally brought up that night—and admitted that she'd broken my heart. I think she'd already known. She said she'd been confused back then, "and who wasn't," she noted. "…But we could have had a good life," she added, finally.

And somehow, that line made all the difference—that it hadn't just been me. It was real, and she had felt it too. That time and place, in a little canyon cottage, had come and gone, forever lost now. But there it was, all that might have been… there in writing.

St. James Infirmary

My father was hosting this time, one of a rotating series of 1960s Business School faculty parties—gatherings straight out of *Mad Men*. There was a full wet bar: liquor bottles in rainbows of color, chrome martini shaker, jigger, spoons, strainers, a crystal ice bucket, green stuffed olives, baby pearl onions, and hand-blown martini glasses from Venice.

My mother arranged the hors d'oeuvres as the first guests were about to arrive—glass and chrome clattering against one another. She was, and always had been, a loner. "This is part of my *job*," my father said defensively, sensing her mood. My mother said nothing. "And this is the life you chose when you married me," he continued. She stared back, sipping a straight gin over ice, and already halfway through it.

At the back corner of the living room, a half-finished oil painting rested on a pinewood easel. Painting was the last remnant of the Greenwich Village bohemian life she'd left behind—that, and listening to the black folk singer Josh White, who had dated her Village roommate.

The oil painting featured a not entirely attractive young woman staring seductively out at the viewer, with full, pendulous breasts, her legs crossed, and a thick bush of pubic hair at the apex. "For God's sake," my father said, suddenly noticing the canvas within the visual of the room. "You've got to cover that thing up. If someone asks to see it, then fine, but don't shove it in everyone's face."

Wordlessly, my mother positioned a drop cloth over the canvas, the model's bare ankles still visible at the bottom. She put on a Josh White record, the oak stereo console booming-out "St. James Infirmary" — "*It was down by old Joe's barroom, on the corner of the square, they were serving drinks as usual, and the usual crowd was there.*" Her hips swayed almost imperceptibly to the words and the bluesy guitar bends, as she made her way back to arranging the hors d'oeuvres.

My father had hired the college-age son of a neighbor to bartend. Vance was a former high-school football jock, all crew cut, biceps, and muscled neck. The party was soon in full swing, and the faculty wives drank up Vance's testosterone-fueled attentions as he poured their elixirs—putting on a show with the chrome martini shaker, holding their hungry gazes.

Vance's younger brother was in my high school class, so we knew one another. "Hey, kid," he said, as I passed by, motioning me over. There was a glint in his eye. He grabbed an opaque plastic cup, pouring me several shots of sherry. "Mum's the word," he said. I nodded, relishing our secret camaraderie. Walking off, I took a sip. It went down easy.

I was soon pleasantly high, drifting through the sea of plaid jackets and summer dresses, taking in the mindless adult chatter as if transmissions from space. Emboldened by the sherry, I decided to take the party up a notch. I faded down Sinatra on the stereo, and substituted the Jimi Hendrix Experience, expecting my father to intervene within seconds. But no one did. I cranked up the bass, giving it some extra bottom.

"Good pick," said a husky female voice. Professor Benson's young wife Joyce knelt down beside me at the stereo. I could feel her hot breath on me, sweet with some indistinct liquor. "They should have put you in charge of the music all along," she smiled, dragging on her cigarette. She looked at me in a way that I'd never experienced with a woman. I could tell that she was high as well. I turned from her probing eyes, pretending to adjust the sound. I'd already finished the cup of sherry, and was now on a second, courtesy of Vance.

Joyce continued talking, but her words were increasingly incomprehensible, drifting over one another in my drunken mind. She touched her hand to my calf, emphasizing some point she'd been making, and I felt electricity go through me. I closed my eyes for a moment, and the room began to spin. I tried to stand up, grabbing the edge of the stereo cabinet. The whole thing began to lurch forward, almost going onto the floor. But I righted it in time. I looked up, and Joyce was gone.

My college-age brother was wearing his best paisley shirt, tan slacks, and penny loafers—trying to appear more adult than he really was. I watched him across the room, in animated conversation with Professor Abelson…who quietly smoked a pipe, taking in my brother's impassioned expositions on the "military industrial complex" and the American "war machine." But from my brother's slurred words, and the exaggerated tone in his voice, I could tell he was also high. I made momentary eye contact with Vance, who was watching my brother from behind the bar. He gave me a conspiratorial thumbs-up.

My father worked the room like a king—flattering the faculty wives, freshening the drinks of colleagues, and leaving a trail of raucous laughter in his wake. My mother stood in a far corner, nursing a highball, observing the gathering like an alien anthropologist.

Needing to pee, I headed down the long hall past the

bedroom I shared with my brother. I found the bathroom door inexplicably half-open—the light on, and the fan humming. Peering in, I saw my brother slumped over on the toilet, his pants around his feet. Panicked, I glanced down the hall, wondering how many might have passed by. Stepping back into the room, I closed and locked the door. I nudged my brother, but he merely groaned. Looking down, I discovered that he'd vomited in the cloth bowl of his cotton briefs—a hardening gray sludge of shrimp hors d'oeuvres.

Closing the door back behind me, I went in frantic search of my mother—finding her in conversation with my father's colleague, Bob Dickerson, a former college football star, and now sports memorabilia entrepreneur. She seemed unusually animated around Dickerson, laughing at his jokes in a way that I knew was forced and out-of-character. She lightly touched his bare forearm, offering to freshen his drink.

I followed her to the bar. "I need your help," I said, urgently.

"I'm busy," she replied evenly, adding ice to Dickerson's glass.

"I'm serious," I insisted. "There's been an accident in the bathroom, with Mike." She looked at me in disbelief.

"Goddammit," she hissed, "can't I *ever* have any enjoyment in life?" She made her way back to Dickerson with the drink, telling him that she'd be right back.

We slipped into the bathroom, and together managed to get the soiled underpants off of my brother, wrapping his lower half in a large smiley face beach towel. I scanned the hall outside, making sure the coast was clear, then motioned to my mother. Supporting him on either side, we made it to my and my brother's bedroom, laying him on the nearest mattress—

mine. The minute he hit the sheets, another paroxysm of vomit came—more gray sludge, and in great volumes, running down the wall alongside my bed.

My mother returned with a wet towel, cleaning up the mess—looking angrier than I'd ever seen her. My brother was soon passed out again, sprawled across the bed. She stared down at him, strangely expressionless.

"I have to get back to the party," she said. I knew that she wanted to get back to Dickerson.

Still high myself, I lay on my brother's bed, closing my eyes. I felt as if I was hurtling backward, at an ever-increasing speed. Opening my eyes to make it stop, I put on an 8-track tape of Pink Floyd, the ethereal strains washing over the moonlit room.

I stared up at the '60s psychedelic poster on the wall above my brother—concentric Day-Glo orange rectangles on solid black, receding into a distant infinity. My parents had gotten it for me during a weekend trip to San Francisco. At the center of the smallest rectangle, in block letters, it had said— "LOVE." But I found it corny and uncool, almost embarrassing to have on my wall. So I thanked them, then cut out a similarly sized image from a magazine—of the 2001 astronaut who'd been murdered by HAL, his lifeless body drifting in space. I taped the image over the word Love.

* * *

I must have dozed off. I woke to my mother's voice from the other room, saying goodnight to the various guests. I stepped out into the hall. Vance had already been paid and sent home. My father and several of the other professors had gone for a walk down at the seaside cliffs, the wives planning to pick them up there later.

Joyce threaded her way through the crowd to my side, complementing me again on my musical taste, her hand soft in mine. "I really enjoyed talking with you," she said, looking me in the eye.

Dickerson had inexplicably remained behind. As everyone filed out the door, he thanked my mother for "a wonderful evening," taking her by the hand. He kissed her on the cheek, and she turned into it.

After the last of the guests had left, my mother turned to me with fire in her eyes. She made her way back to the bedroom, angrily shaking my brother awake. He looked momentarily stunned and disoriented, scanning the darkened room, awareness slowly coming into his eyes.

"Goddamn you!" she screamed. "You threw-up all over the bathroom, all over the wall here, and God knows who might have seen you! Do you know what that could do to your father's career?" His eyes suddenly narrowed, anger rising in them. He seemed strangely energized by her outburst. He got out of the bed. Tossing the towel aside, he put on a pair of blue jeans with no underwear, oblivious to my mother's presence.

"What do you care about his career, anyway?" he shot back. "Other than this house, and the life it brings you!"

He wandered out to the living room, eyeing the bombed-out remnants of the party—half-eaten hors d'oeuvres, pieces of olives and cheese cubes on toothpicks, glasses scattered everywhere. My mother followed after, still not done with him.

For some reason, my brother suddenly focused on my mother's painting in the back corner. From repeated surreptitious viewings by the men at the party, the drop cloth now exposed a good half of the painting, including a large breast. He eyed the canvas for a moment then pulled the cloth entirely away, tossing it to the floor.

He'd always hated her nudes, was embarrassed to have his friends over because of them. He circled the easel in mock admiration. "Such delicate brush strokes, such *artistry!*" he said, leaning-in close. He looked back at my mother.

"You know," he mused professorially, "in the future, they'll just connect electrodes to your head, and ideas like this will appear on a computer screen, fully formed." He snapped his finger close in front of her face. "Like *that!*"

She stared back at him, expressionless.

"You save the image, and you're done," he continued, looking intently at her, as if waiting for full comprehension of his boozy predictions. And then he went in for the kill. "...Only, a hell of a lot better than this shit."

"You bastard!" she said, slapping him.

He appeared stunned and momentarily disoriented, clearly still half-drunk. Rage began to rise in him. Still barefoot, he glowered back at her, then defiantly stomped on a clear plastic trash can alongside the wet bar. The hard plastic pieces shot out across the tile floor. But then his expression suddenly changed—from drunken confusion, to horror. The three of us looked down, as a dark pool of blood began growing outward from his big toe.

My mother sat him down on a nearby chair, then grabbed another chair and propped up his leg—to get a better look, and to elevate the foot. My brother's face blanched, his eyes becoming glazed and unfocused.

She pressured a white washcloth around the toe. It

quickly soaked red. Unwrapping the cloth, we caught a brief glimpse of the cut before it was drowned in more blood—a surgically precise V-shaped incision, and inside, what looked like tendons. My mother grabbed several more fresh washcloths, telling him to press one around the toe, panic rising in her voice.

Together, we helped him down the stairs to the ground-floor garage, knowing that we had to get to an ER, and soon. Descending the staircase, I felt my brother getting heavier and heavier. I glanced up, and saw a far-away look in his eyes.

A large scrubby field lay just beyond our driveway. As my mother backed out of the garage, our headlights swept the far wall. Small black scorpions peppered the stucco. As we drove away, I imagined them watching us.

* * *

Several hours and ten stitches later, we returned home. It was just after 2 AM. The ER doctor said that my brother had lost so much blood, they'd considered a transfusion. Pulling back into the garage, the scorpions were still there—waiting, watching. My mother killed the engine, heaving a long sigh, her hands still tight on the wheel.

We helped my brother back up the stairs, his foot heavily bandaged now. My father was back from the moonlit walk with his buddies—his checkered sport coat draped across the Davenport sofa. My mother peered into their bedroom, but he was fast asleep. She guided my brother into bed, gently arranging the covers over his foot so as to not apply pressure. She looked down at him for a long moment in the semi-dark, and then softly kissed him on the forehead. "I'm glad you're OK, sweetie," she said, with genuine tenderness.

"Thanks a lot, Mom," he said, his voice nearly cracking.

"Good night, you two," she said finally, turning off the light.

"Good night, Mom," I said.

My brother fell into an exhausted oblivion, and soon began snoring. But I couldn't sleep. I heard my mother stacking dishes in the kitchen sink. There in the moonlit bedroom, I stared up at my poster, and the image at the center. I imagined myself adrift in space—solitary and peaceful—in search of the monolith, and whatever might lay beyond.

And then, through the closed door, I heard the sad faint strains of "St. James Infirmary" on the living room stereo, my mother's voice softly singing along.

The Ranch

Vickie's girlfriend Connie first told her about the place—a beautiful, sprawling horse ranch nestled in the scrub hills above Northridge. As they slammed their school lockers shut that day, Vickie thought…this has to have something to do with boys.

And then, sure enough—"There are a couple of *really* hot guys that ride there," said Connie. But she also warned that "a bunch of weird hippies" had recently moved onto the property.

Vickie just thought—so what else was new, it was 1969. Besides, she liked the idea, of maybe meeting a wild hippie boy. It beat cruising the malls with Connie, and endlessly flirting with the same stuck-up jocks from their school.

That next Saturday, she borrowed her father's Country Squire wagon, winding up the narrow, curling roads off the 405. Connie told her the ranch had once been a set for movies and TV shows—*Bonanza*, and *The Lone Ranger*. She said there was an old man who owned and ran the place, but that the hippies had apparently moved in and taken over when he'd gotten too infirm to handle things on his own.

She edged the Squire through the rutted dirt lot, a plume of dust rising skyward. Peasant-bloused teen girls milled aimlessly about. They reminded Connie of the "stoners" at her school. And then there were a few young men in jeans and tight tee shirts…one of them definitely hot.

A man about her father's age walked purposefully by—in worn-jeans, with long scraggly hair and an unkempt beard. As she slowed the car, he glanced back—a look you gave when you knew someone, or wanted to. Instinctively, Vickie turned away.

She parked alongside a ramshackle barn, a weathered wooden sign out front reading, "Office." It was cool and dark inside, the heat of the day and the drone of the cicadas like dreams kept at bay. An old man at the counter turned as she entered. But his eyes seemed oddly vacant, staring out into the distance. He asked what she was there for.

"Um, I wanted to rent a horse, and to ride," she said.

"Oh, okay," he nodded slowly, as if that wasn't the only possible answer. His mottled hands probed at the countertop, finally finding an old bound ledger, and then sliding it toward him.

He offered Connie a pen, his hand shaking and unsteady, telling her to enter her address and license number. Then he took payment for a two-hour ride, stuffing the bills in his oily pant pocket.

One of the peasant-bloused girls entered just then, and glanced knowingly at the old man. Without asking, the girl grabbed a can of beer from a small humming refrigerator, cracked it open, then headed back out—cocking a jeaned hip at him before blowing a parting cheesecake kiss. But the old man seemed not to notice, his eyes forever distant.

Vickie picked out a saddle and bridle from a row of worn metal hooks lining the sidewall. Then the young man she'd seen outside led her to the stables, hauling her gear effortlessly over his broad shoulders. He was barely older than Vickie— with a coltish stride, and eyes that seemed kind and somehow knowing. She was glad now that she hadn't come with Connie, who prided herself on stealing boys.

The young man's legs were so long, it was hard for

Vickie to keep up. But then he glanced back and slowed, asking her name—and with cute dimples when he smiled. Rounding the corner, they passed the man with the dark beard, his gaze on her once more. The young man had been telling Connie all about his favorite trails, but he stopped in mid-sentence.

She selected a brown mare, and the boy saddled it for her. Standing close by he unfolded a ranch map, continuing with his favorite trails, and reminding her she had a two-hour rental. Cinching the saddle one last time, he inadvertently brushed up against Vickie's hip, smiling shyly. There were those dimples again. As she trotted away, Vickie glanced back.

It was a beautiful L.A. day—the sky cloudless, and almost painfully blue. The ranch was everything Connie had promised—majestic winding trails, and enormous rock formations like ancient stone sentinels. A hawk drifted lazily overhead, before finally descending down a long, narrow ravine. The meditative drone of the cicadas seemed to come from all directions at once.

Vickie gazed out at the rolling brown hills, past a wiry scrub oak. In the distance, she caught a vista of the San Fernando Valley below, and tried to spot her neighborhood. She had told her father she'd be at the mall all day with Connie. She knew he wouldn't like her young ranch hand. But she did.

* * *

Checking her watch, Vickie suddenly realized the rental time was nearly up. It was already well into the heat of the day, so she made sure to cool the mare down on the long ride back—taking one of the more level trails, and then walking the last half-mile. Descending the final switchback before the ranch below, she checked her purse for a pen and paper, in case she saw the boy again.

But he was nowhere to be found, the stables deserted. She tied the horse at the worn posts outside the office barn. Scanning the cool dark interior, her eyes slowly adjusting, she spotted a man in the shadows at a far corner. He was mid-20s, a wiry red mustache, and eyes that felt hard and somehow calculating.

Vickie told him her horse was outside, and that she had already paid. He opened the ledger, running his finger down the day's entries. "I don't show any payment," he said, in a Texas drawl.

"Well, I did!" she said.

Without responding, he went out to check the horse, and then returned a moment later. "You didn't cool her down," he said, "and now one of us is gonna have to do it for you. There's a $15 fee for that."

Vickie said she'd been riding for years, and had indeed cooled the horse down. The man just stared back.

"I already paid for the ride, and I'm not going to pay more for something I didn't even do," she blurted out. But her words felt foolish, childish. Wanting to take charge, she grabbed her purse, heading out into the blinding light.

The man started after, soon followed by several of the girls. The cicadas whispered in unison, coming at her from all sides now. Walking faster, Vickie fumbled with her keys, frantically unlocking the car door, getting in, re-locking it from inside, and then turning the ignition. But the engine merely groaned in the sweltering heat.

The man and the girls soon surrounded the car, and then

began violently rocking it from side-to-side. It was as if they had wordlessly become some synchronized machine, working toward some unknown task.

Vickie stared out at the haunted faces surrounding her. She considered bolting and running, but to where?

She'd left the passenger window half rolled-down during her ride, to keep the car cooler inside. One of the girls suddenly reached-in, grabbed her purse from the seat, and then tore away with it.

"Stop! Stop!" Vickie screamed, tears welling in her eyes. The car continued to rock, ever more violently. Real tears began to flow now.

But then suddenly, her young man was there alongside the car—the purse in his hand. He motioned for Vickie to roll the window back down, urging her on with his eyes.

Cautiously, she obeyed. As if having received a mental communication, the others stepped back. The rocking ceased.

"Here's your purse," he said gently, handing it in to her. His eyes were kind, but urgent now. He leaned in closer. "Don't ever come back here," he whispered.

She nodded blankly, set the purse on the seat beside her, finally managed to get the car going, and then slowly pulled away. Still shaking, Vickie glanced in the rear view mirror. Inexplicably, the others began to wander off. But through a rising plume of dust, she saw the young man still watching her, his face impossible to read.

* * *

Vickie and Connie went to the mall that next weekend—

the same boring boys, and Connie doing what she always did. Vickie hadn't told anyone about the ranch, not even Connie.

She wanted to see the boy again, maybe to thank him. But she didn't dare go back. She'd had a dream about him the other night—where they *did* things to one another. He knew her now in ways that no one ever had.

A few weeks later, she was watching the evening TV news with her father. A report came on describing how a band of hippies had invaded a hillside home, brutally murdering several Hollywood stars. The camera footage suddenly cut to an aerial shot of a horse ranch in the San Fernando foothills...and then mug shots of the hippies.

Staring at the faces on the flickering TV screen, Vickie recognized every one. And there at the center, the young man who had saddled her horse—his eyes boring down into her.

Vickie's father glanced over, catching her expression. "I'm sorry, Princess. My God, what a world."

He grabbed the TV remote, but the story was on nearly every channel. He finally landed on *Gilligan's Island*—Gilligan and the Skipper were at it again.

"There, that's better," her father said, looking over, and then patting her on the knee.

But Vickie just continued staring, no longer even seeing. She suddenly heard cicadas droning outside the open living room window.

"Are you alright, sweetheart?" her father asked, finally. "Was it that story?"

She still said nothing.

He paused. "You really haven't seemed yourself lately. Is anything wrong? Is it something at school?"

But then his face brightened, and he turned to her. "I bet I know," he smiled. "...Is it a boy?"

Balboa

I knew someone once who was briefly a heroin addict. He explained, with almost fondness, the simplicity of his life during that time. All that mattered, he said, was figuring out how and where to get your next fix. Everything else became incidental. And while it eventually descended into an all-consuming hell, for a time it had an almost Zen-like quality of peeling away the non-essentials of life, down to the laser intensity of that single path and that single goal.

There was a time and a life for me that felt similar—a daily routine of supreme simplicity. I had no friends, no girlfriend, not even the occasional date. I similarly had no television, and no phone. I slept on a used mattress on the floor of a weathered, seaside studio cottage, with a single wooden chair in the corner of the small dim room.

I got up early each morning, bought a donut and a cup of "Kona Coffee" at the nearby Winchell's, and then drove my battered VW bug onto the small ferry boat landing of the Balboa Peninsula. The ten-minute ferry crossing was my morning ritual and retreat—out on deck with a steaming coffee, taking in the sea air, the rhythmic chug of the ship's engine, the churn of the water, the gulls wheeling overhead.

Then I drove to campus, attended classes, and when I wasn't in class, studied in the library, a cloistered world under white-hot fluorescence. The courses were demanding—a single, one-unit chemistry lab requiring four in-lab hours each week, and then a good eight hours of prep work and lab reports. And there were many such classes. I ate alone in the cafeteria—sometimes people watching, but with no human interaction beyond day-to-day business, and in-class academics.

That routine spanned from 9 AM to 11 PM, and typically six days a week. At 11 PM, I'd head back to the ferry landing on Balboa Island, to catch the last crossing to the peninsula. The night air was bracing, energizing. I stood out on deck once more, watching the cold city lights recede.

In the hour or so before bed, I'd brew a cup of hot tea, sit cross-legged, and play a silver flute in the dark. And then before drifting off, I'd lie listening to FM radio on headphones—late-night underground rock, or Alan Watts lectures.

I had one set of plates, one set of silverware, and one ceramic coffee cup. The back entrance to the apartment was an ill-fitting wooden screen door, which sometimes made it cold at night, or rattled in the wind. But I never thought to complain, or to change things. I wasn't worried about being robbed, because I barely owned anything, and anyone breaking in might almost wonder whether someone actually lived there. When I wasn't home, I stashed my flute and my radio-headphones in a high nook of the closet, behind a rough wool blanket.

I knew none of my neighbors in the cluster of beach cottages, and spoke to no one. Just down the block was a carnival midway, with a Ferris wheel and amusement park rides—bustling at night with bright neon and laughter, milling children, and couples holding hands. And then two blocks in the other direction, a beautiful and expansive sandy beach—perfect for contemplative walks. But during the entire several quarters I lived there, I never visited either place—not once. Looking back, it almost seems a form of madness.

And then at the end of that year, something shifted. I don't know what, or why. I suddenly recognized that time of my life had ended. "I thought you were going to stay," the landlady told me. "So did I," I replied.

Scanning the bare dim room one last time, I placed the lone wooden chair alongside the bed, in case the next resident had visitors. Then I turned out the light, locked the door, and came down from the mountaintop, returning to the world.

I walked out to the nearby beach, standing alone along the shore, staring out to sea. A formation of brown pelicans skimmed low across the sparkling water, almost touching the surface at times. Suddenly, one dropped away from the group, falling like an arrow, disappearing into the dark waters—and then emerging once more, fresh and alive, a writhing silver fish held tight in its beak.

The Dancer

June takes a breath, preparing. It's a new spot, but the setting looks good…

Finally ready, she darts out into the streaming traffic — cars parting like schooling fish, drivers honking. She dances between the bright headlights, waving, calling out for help.

The freeway overpasses loom like monsters, jeweled office towers rising in the distance. At first there are no takers. Two cars narrowly miss one another, one of them clipping a high curb.

She ups the ante, windmilling her arms, screaming at the top of her lungs — "Help! Someone, please help!" Still, they stream past.

A new-model Tesla finally forces its way across several lanes, slowing to the curb ahead. *God, sometimes she practically has to get herself killed.*

The car's window lowers as she makes her way to them. "Man, am I glad you guys stopped!" June shouts above the traffic.

She sizes up the couple fast—settling on the man. It's more dangerous on the traffic side, but the men are always easier. She dodges over to them across several more lanes, almost getting hit again in the process.

She squats alongside the car, hands on her knees, catching her breath. When she stands again, their eyes are open to her, ready. She's maybe halfway home.

The man alone would be a dunk shot, but the girl may still be a problem. She can see it in the eyes. But there's definitely money here: the car, and little Miss Prissy beside him. From his tousled graying hair, and the pressed tee shirt, she figures—computers.

June stays with the usual, slow and easy—try to seem like one of them. "I was really getting scared," she chokes-up, "thought nobody would ever stop."

She stares in at the girl's soft white sweater, the heart-shaped pendant at the neck—gold and ruby, and maybe even a diamond. *If she could just get to it, the chain would go like thread.* But it could be trouble. Peño has warned her, never reach inside—you lose control that way, maybe even an arm.

"My car broke down on the freeway, and my phone's dead," she recites, looking the man purposefully in the eye. "I've been trying to arrange a tow truck, but these homies keep cruising by, calling me names. I'm really scared!"

June feels the girl focus in on her. Women can be the worst. They see down into you.

She already has the guy, she can tell—but the other is still trouble. She continues on, giving the girl just enough eye. "I need $29.50 for when the tow truck gets here," she tells them. "My purse is back up in the car, but I don't have enough."

She's tried different amounts, but this one's always been the clincher. The fifty cents makes it seem real — and it's close enough to thirty bucks that she usually gets a twenty and a ten. She gives it time to sink in, to let them talk.

But then they start whispering to one another, and for too long. The girl finally leans over to her side—the eyes are newly hard. "Look, we'd really like to help you," she says, "but I've been scammed like this before." *She was so close—fucking little bitch!*

"I swear to you, this is no scam," June says, forcing up tears. She's losing it—even the man. "Look, I work at Chevy's, over by the airport…"

A jolt is what that little bitch needs! Maybe even one to the face—leave something to remember her by. But Peño's told her that people have died that way, too close to the brain. She isn't a murderer.

"I'll be there tomorrow, on the afternoon shift," she continues. "If you come by, I'll pay you then, even give you guys a free dinner!"

It's working, the eyes are softening. She moves in closer to the man, to cinch it—hoping he'll smell her perfume. June pulls out a scrap of paper, begins writing down a random number. The man twists up to one side, reaching into his back pocket, pulling out a fresh twenty and a ten.

She holds his gaze, and even adds a touch of sex to it, hoping Miss Prissy doesn't see. *Who knows, this one could be a repeat donor—maybe get his number somehow.* "Thanks a lot," she says, focusing now on the girl, "you've really saved my ass!"

"Don't mention it," the man says, making clear it's his money. But June hands the scribbled number to the girl. *She and Miss Prissy are practically sisters now.* She takes the bills, careful not to seem too anxious.

She's about to give them her final line and be gone. But then the man says— "Hey, by the way, can I get your driver's license, maybe write down some info?"

Shit!! How could she have never thought of this? They stare back, waiting for an answer. Her hand begins to tremble.

"Um, I can't," she says, finally, but clearly improvising.

She tries to recover the momentum, but has already waited too long. "…I told you, my purse is up in the car," she blurts-out, looking up at the overpass. Fear is rising in their eyes. *They know.* "I can't get to it until the tow truck comes," she continues, even more unconvincingly.

June waits to see what will happen. She's sure the man isn't packing—too soft at the center. The girl might be, though. Looks can be deceiving with women. She edges her hand slowly toward her back pocket. If worse comes to worse, she'll give the guy one to the neck and run for it, hope he survives.

The fear is building in their faces. "OK, well, never mind," the man says, nervously. June watches his eyes go down to her hand, there at the pocket.

As the man puts away his wallet, she hears the muffled latch of the car doors. She sees him eyeing the path ahead, planning a potential high-speed escape. "Good luck," the man says, finally.

In her confusion, she makes eye contact with Miss Prissy—the glare now icy and betrayed. The car's window rises back up—reflecting June's twisted image, and the glittering office towers beyond. They pull away under the crackling orange streetlights.

They'd been all wrong, from the beginning—too old, and too much to lose. Peño has warned her to stick with the younger ones. And that way, if you end up buzzing them, their hearts won't give out.

But some nights, you took what you got.

June fingers the bills. If she'd ended up with just the man, she'd be set now—a damsel in distress, with still-decent looks, and good tits. That was all it took for most guys. And when it really worked, you got them up on the freeway and under the hood of the car—then gave them the juice—a little high-voltage cash-withdrawal. And by the time they came to, you were long gone.

June feels the cold rising up into her now, like a gathering storm from some secret place. She's already spent too much time, and is too drained to do another.

…Thirty fucking dollars for the night. It wasn't much, but enough for a little something. She shivers—already imagining the warming fire in her veins. If she's lucky, and it's decent stuff, it will still be an OK night.

She tucks the bills down her top, and heads to the phones next to Mi-Tee Mart. Peño won't take cell calls—too many footprints.

Afterward she waits, listening to the cars roar by above, imagining it's the ocean. The city lights shimmer like jewels in the day's still-rising heat. A black-and-white edges by in the lanes ahead, but she spots it in time, and ducks into the shadows. *Maybe courtesy of Miss Prissy.*

Peño can usually get to her in a half an hour, and will give her a ride back to the car. After that, she'll have the whole night ahead. Her body already knows what's in store—like a golden light, it will shine down into her, melting away all the cold and all the hardness. She's safe now, for a while. For tonight, the dance is done.

The Apartment

(San Francisco, early-1980s)

She seemed like…such a normal girl.

I'd just moved to the City, and soon discovered Haight Roommate Referral. They had whole notebooks of prospective roommates — with self-ratings on: cleanliness, noisiness, politics, religion, vegetarian/vegan, drug use, sexual orientation.

I found a cool, high-ceilinged, two-bedroom, top-floor flat just off the Panhandle. Valerie's roommate had just moved out with a boyfriend, and the notebook entry said she was open to a guy roommate.

She was cute, in an artsy SF way, but not really my type. And I think she felt the same. She spent most nights at her boyfriend Scotty's place, so it actually worked out great.

But then the landlord raised our rent, by a lot. Two days later, Valerie announced that she was moving in with Scotty. I'd just started a great new job, but I was still trying to save money. I loved the place, and she was almost the perfect roommate — quiet, not crazy, and rarely around. I dreaded having to find someone new, and suggested that maybe I could pay 70% of the new rent, and she could stay and pay just 30%. She looked at me suspiciously. "Why would you want to do that?" she asked. I told her the truth — that it would still help me out rent-wise, and I wouldn't have to find a new roommate. She didn't seem entirely convinced, but finally agreed.

A few days later, she and Scotty dropped by to pick up

her mail. The new rental arrangement soon came up. "That was really nice of you," he said, probing me with intense eyes.

"I'm just glad it worked out," I said matter-of-factly, going through the counter-top stack of mail, separating out Valerie's letters and mine.

She'd told me earlier that Scotty was an aspiring film writer, and was working on a new script idea. For his day job, he was a locksmith. She said that his story centered around a young lock expert who secretly broke into people's homes, then made very subtle changes around their houses. With each new intrusion, his character would up the ante, seeing how long it would take his victims to "get the message" — to recognize what was being done, and then to finally react.

"That's the beauty of it," she'd explained. "It starts out with things that are so small and so subtle, a person might not even notice, or might think they were imagining things, or maybe even come to question their own sanity. The important part," she added, "is what that realization *does* to someone, how they react, and when they finally reach their breaking point."

She seemed very into Scotty, so I agreed it was a good idea. "I guess, write what you know!" I said.

The new rental dynamic worked out great, and I was still able to save a decent amount. But after a month or so, Valerie announced that she was moving out with Scotty after all. "I'm hardly ever here, anyway," she explained.

He came by that weekend to help. After many hours of hauling, they finally headed out with the last load of her stuff. Valerie handed me her key, with what seemed like great ceremony. "Well, see you around," she smiled.

About a week later, I was going through a stack of mail I'd let gather on the kitchen countertop — separating out bills, personal letters, and throwaway ads. Near the bottom, between two junk-mail flyers, I found a small scrap of torn paper, with what looked like female handwriting on it. "Hi, Steve!" it said. My mind raced, replaying how long it might have been there, versus when Valerie had moved out. I couldn't say for sure, tossed-out the note, and soon forgot all about it.

Around that same time, I'd started dating a new girl in the neighborhood, and she eventually spent the night. Before we finally settled in, she got up to pee. Crawling back under the covers, she said — "I never figured you for the kind of guy that would put that blue chemical stuff in your toilet."

"Um, I'm not," I said.

She looked back at me. "Well, go look."

Sure enough, the bowl water was a deep electric blue — and it hadn't been that morning. I pulled off the porcelain top. There was a Ty-D-Bol device hanging inside. I got back into bed, saying I had no idea how it had gotten there.

"Couldn't it be your landlord?" she asked.

"He lives out of state," I said.

"Well…maybe it was there all along," she suggested, "it ran low, and then the last bit dribbled out today."

"The thing looks totally full," I reported. She looked back at me with worried eyes.

A few days later, I was going through a new stack of mail on the counter top. I once again found a scrap of paper between some ads. It was even smaller than the first, with a single hand-drawn red heart on it. I looked to the front door, and then checked the kitchen cabinet for Valerie's key. It was right where I'd stashed it.

I came home from work several nights later. Closing the door, I suddenly realized that the whole apartment smelled like the noxious model airplane glue of my childhood. I went from room to room, trying to locate the source. But it seemed to be everywhere — and so powerful, it burned my eyes. I opened all the windows, and then went out to dinner. When I came back, things seemed better, so I shrugged it off, closed the windows, got into bed, and soon fell asleep. But in the middle of the night I woke up and realized that the smell was back, and *really* bad.

For the next several days I kept all the windows open while I was at work, and then closed them when I got back home — seeing whether the smell ever dissipated. It didn't. I asked my neighbors on either side whether they'd noticed "a chemical smell," or had perhaps been doing repair work. They didn't/hadn't, and looked at me strangely.

My new girlfriend once again came to spend the night. At the door, I told her about the glue situation. She listened to my story with doubt...and a bit of fear in her eyes. But once inside, she agreed that it was real, and pretty bad. It was a cold and foggy night. I explained that we should probably keep the bedside window open in spite of the fog, to dampen-down the fumes. I got us an extra blanket from the hall closet. "I hope those fumes don't damage my eggs," she half-joked, trying to lighten the mood.

She got up to pee in the middle of the night, and then shook me awake. The toilet water was now green.

In the morning, she seemed preoccupied, gave me a peck on the cheek, and then headed off to work. Later that day, she called me at my office. "Look, I really like you," she said. "But there are just too many weird things going on in your life... that you should probably work on." Her voice trailed off. "So, I guess I'll...talk to you," she said, finally. And then the line went dead.

A week later, an underground transformer vault

exploded outside my downtown office building, blanketing the area in a mist of electrical oil. The high-rise was soon evacuated by the fire department, and we were all sent home.

On the dinner-hour news that night, PG&E reassured the public that it was nothing to be concerned about, and that they were investigating the cause of the explosion. But a suspicious reporter had the oil residue tested at a lab, and within hours determined that it contained high levels of PCBs — a known carcinogen and neurotoxin. On the late news that night, I watched a klieg-lit scene outside my building, with HazMat men in space suits steam-cleaning the cordoned-off area. The SF public health director, lab report in hand, told an on-scene reporter that anyone who had been within the vicinity of the incident should bag-up their clothing, and surrender it to the city for testing and toxic disposal.

The building remained closed for several more days until they could fully decontaminate the area. I bagged-up my work clothes, and dropped them off at the public health department. That night, while taking-off my socks, I discovered that a layer of skin on the soles of both feet was peeling-off — like sheets of plastic. I wondered if it was from the PCBs.

Getting ready for bed, I opened all the windows to air out the glue fumes. On one windowpane, there was a small rainbow colored butterfly sticker. It hadn't been there before. Then I went to pee, the water was now purple.

I turned on the radio, and lay there staring at the ceiling. The station was playing, "Shock the Monkey." I wondered what else Scotty might have in store, how far it would all go…and when the movie would end.

Twinkle, Twinkle, Little Star

We had been many things across the years—friends, lovers, mysterious others, and now long-distance caregiver/confidant on my part. I sat there in the dark, talking with her by phone.

"What does *cyanotic* mean?" she asked, after a long pause.

"Why do you wonder?" I replied.

"It's what the ER doctors said as I hovered over the room, watching them work on me."

I explained that it meant turning blue, from a lack of oxygen.

"...There was all kinds of frantic activity," she mused, "people scrambling around, and then one of them shouted to the others, 'she's cyanotic!' And then things seemed to get even crazier. At least, that's the way it looked from up there."

I didn't know what to say, and stayed quiet.

"But then something changed," she continued. "All of a sudden, they didn't seem as concerned. I had the impression that a crisis of some sort had passed. And then at that same moment, it was as if some powerful magnetic force was pulling me back down to the gurney, and I was suddenly back in my body, whole again."

That was what she told me afterward, in a long late-night call after she'd gotten back from the hospital. It had been a severe heart attack, she said, nearly fatal—the result of decades of vascular damage from diabetes.

"But it was beautiful," she reported, as if recounting some exotic vacation. "It was just like they always say—a tunnel of brilliant white light, more pure than you can even imagine, and a supreme sense of inner peace."

She paused. "…I don't want to die, because there are still a lot of things I want to do in life," she said. "But I'm not afraid of it anymore—not at all."

* * *

But then a few days later, while I was out of town on business, a second heart attack came. Her mother was there with her in San Francisco, and knew that things were not good— wanted to dial 911. Begged, in fact. But she forbade it, shaking her head vehemently during moments of lucidity.

She made it through much of the night. And then at dawn, the end came.

When I got home from my weekend away, her mother's message was on the machine. Even though it shouldn't have been a shock, it still was—profoundly so. I sat there in the dark with my wife, the two of us talking, trying to take it all in.

On the far bookshelf was a baby boom box that she had bought for our newborn son. It was remote-controlled, but both the device and the controller were sitting together on a top shelf, far from anything.

It still felt almost beyond belief, that she was gone. She seemed to know things about people, and about the future, that defied possibility. She'd declared with certainty that I would not have twins as indicated by an early ultrasound, but only a single baby, a boy. And she had been right.

We sat there for a long time, my wife and I—talking, thinking of her, but finally at a loss for words. And then suddenly, the baby boom box turned-on, lighting-up the dark room, and playing a nursery rhyme—"Twinkle, Twinkle, Little Star."

It had never done that before...and it never did again.

(For Christine)

Nude Popcorn

Campus housing said it could be weeks, maybe even months, before they could get me a room in the dorms. It was my freshman year at USC. My older brother was in his final year, and living off campus in a run-down, two-story hippie pad. Soon out of any other viable options, my parents pressured him into letting me crash on a camping cot in his small bedroom.

Almost everyone in the house was a cinema major, which seemed to entail hanging out, playing music, getting high, and making the occasional experimental film. Meanwhile, I was taking calculus and physics, and slowly dying on the academic vine.

But things were way more interesting on the home front…

The kitchen sink of the place was perpetually filled with crusted, dirty dishes, so the whole downstairs was crawling with cockroaches. You didn't want to enter a room at night and suddenly flip on a light switch.

The usual off-the-shelf remedies, like Black Flag, had already been tried, but failed miserably. In desperation, one of the disgusted young women roommates went to the local drug store, begging for help. The pharmacist there referred her to an exterminator friend, who provided a mysterious controlled substance white powder. The man instructed her that a single spoonful—but no more!—should be mixed with a quart of water, and then sloshed around the baseboards of the kitchen and the dining room area. "This will take care of your problem," he nodded, smiling fiendishly.

That afternoon, several curious roommates gathered to watch the application. At first, there was nothing. "This is bullshit, man!" someone said, after many long minutes of waiting. But then a low-rumble began to build within the woodwork, followed by a literal wave of frantic scuttling roaches washing out across the worn linoleum floor. Women and men alike scrambled onto nearby chairs and tables, some of them screaming in horror as the roach death-throes played out below.

* * *

And then someone left out the bowl of mescaline-laced green Jell-O. The house-dog, Soaring Hawk, got into it at the kitchen table, licking it nearly clean. Freaked and agitated, he paced from room to room, scanning our assembled worried faces with haunted, electric eyes—before finally dashing out the back door as someone re-entered after emptying the trash.

The whole house was in mourning for days. Tom, who'd made the Jell-O, was inconsolable. "I should have been more careful...I should have been more careful," he muttered over and over to himself, "poor little guy." The women of the house, in their denim overalls, gathered each night at the back stoop, a solemn sisterhood vigil, sing-songing, *"Soaring-Hawk!"* But he was never seen again.

* * *

A week or so later, I came home late from a hard day of calculus homework. The living room and dining room were both dark, but a spectral white light glowed from the distant kitchen, brighter than day. Tentatively entering the room, I found it filled with movie klieg lights, a tripod-mounted 16 mm movie camera, and a long-haired assistant holding a boom mic above the elaborate scene.

Seeing me enter, the soundman held a finger to his lips, and then quickly returned to his task. At the stove, a stark-naked young woman cooked Jiffy Pop, her hips gyrating seductively with each rotation of the pan, a steaming aluminum-foil mushroom rising with the building clatter of the hot corn.

After a minute or so, the girl's hips gradually slowed, and the metallic cacophony sputtered and pinged down to an eerie silence—the foil dome looming large and full. The girl turned down the blue flame, then seized a gleaming nearby kitchen knife, ceremoniously stabbing the foil, lowering her face, and taking in the rising buttery cloud of steam. She turned to the camera, knife still in hand, eyes filled with satisfied desire.

"…And, cut!" said the young director.

"Well, that was something different," I said to the guy who'd silenced me.

"It's called, *Jiffy Pop*," he reported.

"Looks more like *Nude Popcorn*," I said.

His eyes brightened. "Hey, that's not bad! I'll mention it to Tom."

* * *

It was endlessly hard to sleep at the place. Lying there on my foldout cot that first night, shafts of strobing white-hot light suddenly erupted across the sheet hung as a makeshift curtain. "What the hell *is* that?" I asked my brother.

"It's just the guy next door," he reported matter-of-factly. "He deals in stolen cars, cuts them up at night with an acetylene torch, and then sells the parts on the black market."

"Ah," I said.

Everyone in the neighborhood seemingly had a racket. The local kids ran a ring of stolen bikes from campus, re-selling them to other unwitting students. And a full-on, armed drug dealer lived out back in the granny unit above the carriage-style garage.

And there were ever-shifting turf wars between the various camps. Incensed one afternoon as the kids brazenly cut a bike deal out at the sidewalk—a fat wad of bills clearly in-hand—the drug dealer stormed out with his sawed-off shotgun, telling them to "get the hell away from my house!"

The kids all scattered, but then came back later that night, doused the dealer's VW Bug in gasoline, and flicked a match to it. An enormous fireball soon lit up the night. Within minutes a roaring fire engine arrived, hosed-down the flaming debris, and the blackened shell of the car was hauled away for scrap.

* * *

After that, things calmed down for a bit, but then the real heat arrived. I came home late one night from the library, and Rachel, one of the women cinema majors, exclaimed—"You won't believe what happened today…the FBI was here!"

She said that an undercover agent had come to the door, introduced himself, displayed his badge, and then pulled out a grainy black-and-white telephoto picture from a manila folder. "Do you know this man?" he asked, officiously. The figure was clearly the car guy next door.

She guessed that it would be pointless to lie. "Um, yeah, he's our neighbor," she said, "but I don't really *know* him."

The agent nodded, then pulled out a second 8x10 photo—featuring Rachel and the man, laughing together on our front lawn. "Is this you?" he asked rhetorically, his eyes probing.

Sensing her growing fear, he explained that the man had recently expanded his operation into neighboring states, which made it a federal crime—and that they'd been surveilling the area for days. "Anyone knowingly aiding and abetting him could ultimately be considered an accessory to his crimes," he noted.

Rachel paused. "Look, I know he may be up to some shady stuff," she said, "but I don't really know him, or what he does, beyond just saying hello from time to time. I'm just a student."

The agent looked back at her for a long time, nodded, and then put away the pictures. "I'd appreciate it if you didn't mention this conversation," he said. She nodded back.

Soon after, the car thief disappeared into the night, along with his backyard of cars and parts. Perhaps he'd gotten wind of things—maybe even from Rachel. She never really said, and no one wanted to ask. But it was a whole lot easier to sleep at night without that blowtorch.

I later heard that *Nude Popcorn* was the hit of the

semester at the Cinema Department's student shorts program —
proclaimed as a tour de force exploration of psycho-sexual,
post-feminist, political dialectics.

The film had been dedicated to "Soaring Hawk." And a
sequel was in the works.

Petra

Paris/Berlin, early-1980s

My brother had taken to his sickbed, there in our little Left Bank hotel room.

We'd gotten unpaid leaves from our L.A. software jobs to become Paris buskers, for who knew how long. And it had worked out incredibly well. Each afternoon, we'd head down into a Metro station for several hours—set up a battery-powered Pignose amp, plug in my Fender Strat, and then I'd let loose while my brother belted out the vocals: Neil Young, Clash, Cars, Elvis Costello, and the real Elvis. The tile-walled acoustics made even so-so performances sound amazing, and the Europeans seemed to actually respect you for doing what you did—often paying our bills for the day.

But it was an unseasonably cold and rainy summer, and our room had only a small steam radiator. My brother soon developed a barking, croup-like cough. Within days, he was reduced to two pitiful eyes peering out from under rough wool covers. I found myself on endless runs to the nearby *Pharmacie*—first a thermometer, then throat lozenges, then various codeine elixirs. And from there, home remedies like apple cider vinegar—God knows what that was about.

For a few days, I took to sightseeing on my own. But returning to the stale dark room one afternoon, he looked like death warmed over. "I just need to get out of this gloom," he wheezed, "to get the chill out of my bones."

I knew I had to do something—it was beginning to feel like a Paul Bowles novel. That afternoon, I headed down to Gare du Nord, and got us an overnight sleeper passage to Nice. Fortunately, my brother was too weak to resist.

* * *

And the change in weather seemed to do the trick. After a few days on the beach in Nice, the color slowly came back into my brother's face, and his cough began to subside.

"The healing properties of the human body are truly amazing," he declared, eyeing a gaggle of twenty-something girls passing by on the sand. "Just days ago, I was near death in Paris, and now look at me!" He paused. "Maybe it was the apple cider vinegar." I just nodded.

In the end, though, Nice proved almost too nice. Sure, there were the topless beaches, and the boardwalk scene, and the casino. But after days of sun and sand, we found ourselves longing for something a little *grittier*.

So we headed to Berlin.

Another overnight train run, lulled to sleep by the rhythm of the rails. After just a few hours, though, we jolted awake to the screech of metal-on-metal, the train rapidly decelerating. Simultaneously, a commotion erupted in the hall outside, rapid-fire voices shouting over one another in different languages.

Peering out the compartment door, I watched as a burly uniformed conductor forcibly shoved a couple down the long carpeted hall. The man wore a pinstriped suit, with a large-brimmed hat tilted at a rakish angle. He was middle aged, jowly, but with an odd, regal air—the sense of a Count having hit a bit of a rough patch. His companion was at least ten years younger—an hourglass figure poured into a form-fitting dinner dress, teetering on strappy heels, with ringlets of raven hair spilling onto her forehead. She looked like trouble in a tube.

A German in our compartment went out to investigate. "They're both drunk," he reported on returning. "The man apparently got into an argument with the conductor, and then pulled a knife. They're being let off at this stop."

We stared out the window to the tracks below. A small boarding platform glowed in the dim train light. And beyond that, scattered farmhouses, surrounded by open grassland fading into the night. It was the middle of nowhere.

The conductor forced the couple down the stairs of the car to the gravel below. Unsteady on her heels, the woman smoothed her hair, and then adjusted her dress—as if about to enter a grand ball. The man calmly lit a fat cigar, waiting to see what might happen next.

The conductor began hurling their luggage out onto the ground. The Count passively watched, his cigar glowing rhythmically. One of the thrown bags came right at him, but he held-up a suited arm, effortlessly deflecting it to one side. His cigar seemed to glow in triumph.

"Wow, what a tough cookie," my brother admired.

And then it was done—the car door slammed shut, and the train lurched forward. I watched the Count and his woman as we passed by, his cigar still glowing in the starry night.

We fell back into a dead sleep for several more hours. But then the train began clattering to a stop once more. I wondered if we had already arrived. But it was still pitch black outside—more bleak grasslands in the moonlight. Staring out the window, I saw legions of ghostly uniformed men, with German Shepherd dogs tugging at leather leashes. Several of the men had rifles slung over their shoulders. They looked like hunters on the prowl. Powerful flashlight beams methodically scoured the undercarriage of the train, car-by-car.

"East German soldiers," explained our compartment-mate, sensing my puzzlement. "They are searching for stowaways before we cross into West Berlin."

The flashlights finally clicked off, and I thought that might be it. But then our compartment door flew open, like a scene from a WWII movie. "Your passports!" a soldier barked at us, a black Makarov pistol holstered at his waist.

We obeyed, silently handing them over. He eyed them one-by-one, stamped them, passed them back, and then continued down the hall.

* * *

I jolted awake once more, disoriented, bleary-eyed from the long night—a slate gray dawn as we clattered into the metal latticework of the Bahnhof-Zoo station. We made our way through the bustling morning commuter crowds—loudspeakers echoing announcements across the vast expanse.

Famished, we ducked into the fluorescent-lit coffee house at the Zoo station's street level, ordering jumbo platters of eggs, potatoes, and sausage. "*Bier?*" asked the waitress, matter-of-factly.

It was 7 AM, but at nearby tables we spotted countless businessmen drinking tall steins with their breakfast. We looked at one another. "Um, sure," I nodded.

Bellies full, we exited out to the high-rise morning bustle of Kurfürstendamm. I had a major beer-buzz going, and it was only 8 AM.

It was too early to claim the room we'd rented, so we wandered the teeming boulevard—past the Kaiser Wilhelm Church Memorial, starkly lit against a stormy indigo sky. The grey stone edifice had been left scarred and ravaged by WWII allied bombing runs, and was now kept that way, frozen in time—a monument to the madness of war.

In our wanderings, we rounded a corner and suddenly came upon the Berlin Wall—twelve feet high, reinforced concrete, and topped with gleaming, coiled razor wire. At regular intervals, wooden platforms with stairs let you see over into the East. The worn, rough-hewn structures looked almost like gallows.

Climbing up and peering over, it was like gazing into a time warp of the 1950s—streets filled with boxy, East German Trabant sedans, lurching and belching exhaust, most painted a drab gray, or in strange foreign pastels.

A hundred feet back from the wall on the east side, a lone soldier stood in a cement watchtower, topped with large and powerful floodlights. The young guard was so close I could actually see his face—his eyes steely, expressionless. He stood at attention, both hands tight on a black Kalashnikov rifle, pointed rigidly skyward. We made sudden eye contact, and I nodded in recognition. But there was no response.

That afternoon, we checked into our room, a steel and glass high-rise hotel, with a stunning view of downtown Berlin—the bustling night traffic of Kurfürstendamm in the distance, and the rotating blue-neon beacon of the Mercedes headquarters.

* * *

Let's Go Berlin had mentioned a cool coffee house/club that featured nightly music. It was the peak of the New Wave '80s, and just after Bowie's Berlin period, so I figured they'd know how to do music right.

The place was packed, smoke-filled, with people necessarily sharing tables. The girl next to us was about our age—long, almost L.A. surfer-blonde hair, with wireframe glasses, and penetrating blue eyes.

"Petra," she smiled, as we sidled into the cramped space. A young, bearded singer was in the middle of an intense song sung in German—his delivery acid and Elvis Costello-like, over New Wave barre chords.

There was something entirely "German" about the song and the cadence, with strange theatrical hints of Brecht-Weil. Sensing my interest, Petra whispered a translation of the chorus. "He says that he will not change his song to make it in Berlin… not one word."

"I like it," I whispered back, "and he shouldn't."

During a break in the music, we learned it was Open Mic night, and that they were still taking sign-ups. "Damn, I wish I'd brought my guitar," I said, "but it's back at the hotel."

Petra asked where we were staying, and seemed to know the area. I could see mental gears turning.

"I'm here on bicycle," she noted. "It's big and it's heavy, and might even work with three. You could sign-up now, and then I could take you guys to get your guitar."

I looked back at her. "Yeah…let's give it a try!" I said.

Petra rode and steered, my brother sat on the handlebars, and I sat on the rack behind—one arm around her waist to keep from falling off, and the other holding my guitar. We cycled past a group of young women, done-up for what seemed a night on the town.

"Meow!" one of them said to us, pawing the air.

"Hookers," explained Petra.

We made it back just in time for our slot. Petra's goateed boyfriend Klaus had just gotten off a late-night University class. He bought us rounds, and then lit up a Gitanes, holding it the German way.

And then it was our turn.

Scanning the smoky blue depths, I hammered out the opening chords of "Psycho Killer," making it extra-raw, rhythmic, letting things ring. The crowd recognized the intro, and began clapping in unison.

My brother prowled the stage like Mick Jagger, hugging the mic with both hands, sometimes going down on one knee, his eyes manic, almost possessed. When we got to the chorus, the crowd joined-in…

> *"Psycho Killer*
> *Qu'est-ce que c'est*
> *Fa-fa-fa-fa-fa-fa-fa-fa-fa-far…"*

It was supposed to be just one song per group, but as we left the stage, the crowd began stamping for an encore. We were halfway back to our seats, but the clatter continued. Petra and Klaus urged us on with their eyes. They seemed to know how things worked.

So we jumped back on stage, and then broke into "Pump It Up." Once again, the crowd joined in on the chorus...

> *"Pump it up...until you can feel it!*
> *Pump it up...when you don't really need it!"*

My brother drew out the lines like Elvis C., belting them at the end — *"Don't really need it! Don't really need it!"*

"That was wonderful!" said Petra, kissing me on the cheek as we came back to our seats. "See, now aren't you glad we got your guitar!"

"I am," I said, still breathless. "Thank you."

She looked back at me with an expression that I still remember — knowing, and longing. I felt her side-glances on me from time to time. But after several more songs, Klaus whispered to her in German, and she whispered something back.

"...We have to go," she said, turning to me, touching my arm. She looked into my eyes.

The four of us hugged. As they headed to the door, Petra glanced back at me, mouthing something I didn't understand. Klaus took her hand, and then they disappeared into the neon night.

It was a long way back, but we were still high from our set. The streets were all but deserted; even the kit-cat girls had called it a night. The high-rise Mercedes sign led our way, a glowing solitary beacon.

* * *

We had a morning train to catch, back to Paris, and decided on a Zoo Station breakfast to tide us over—another early-morning beer buzz. Afterward, there was a good hour to kill before our passage. We wandered the area, once more coming upon the Wall. I kiddingly suggested plugging-in, blasting western rock over to the other side.

"I dunno," said my brother, "I could imagine getting shot from their side, or getting arrested on this side."

"Maybe," I agreed. "But I want to see it again."

We climbed the wooden platform, and to my amazement it was the same watchtower, and the same young guard—his Kalashnikov held rigid. Making eye contact, I could tell he remembered me. Still half-drunk from the breakfast beer, I delivered an off-hand salute, and a loopy smile. The grip relaxed on his rifle. He tried to hide it at first, but then broke into a grin himself, and returned the salute. I bowed, waved goodbye, and headed back down.

We wandered Kurfürstendamm in the gray dawn light, the rush-hour crowds beginning to build. A couple ahead caught my eye—strangely formally dressed for the setting and the hour. They looked ragged around the edges, as if they'd been up all night. Something about the man's gait suddenly clicked. I realized that it was the Count and his woman, from the train.

They'd made it to Berlin after all, and not much had changed. They began arguing in rapid-fire German. She gestured angrily in his face, shouting something, then flicking a thumb at him off her front teeth. He shoved her away, and she staggered back on her heels, almost going down. Regaining her balance, she came back with a vengeance, slapping him hard across the face. He seemed stunned at first, but then it was as if the blow had sobered him up. He burst out laughing, and she began laughing, too. They held hands, and continued down the gray dawn boulevard, her head resting on his caped shoulder.

The morning mists had begun to part, a slowly lifting veil. We passed the Kaiser Wilhelm Memorial, a blood red sun threading the bombed-out pinnacle of the scarred stone church. I thought back to the club last night. And to Petra.

After we'd played, the club owner came over—"The next time you are in Berlin, call me, I will book you!" he'd said. I caught Petra's glance. She smiled sadly, and then Klaus took her hand to go.

And then whatever she had said to me. We never made it back.

Steven Meloan's writing has been seen in *Wired, Rolling Stone, Los Angeles, BUZZ, the San Francisco Chronicle,* and *SF Weekly.* His fiction has appeared in *SOMA Magazine, the Sonoma Valley Sun,* Lummox Press, and Newington Blue Press, as well as at Litquake, Quiet Lightning, and other Bay Area literary events. He has regularly written for the *Huffington Post,* and is co-author of the novel *The Shroud* with his brother Michael. He is a recovered software programmer, and was a street busker in London, Paris, and Berlin.

Instagram: @slmeloan

"Reading these stories, I felt like I was hearing an original voice for the very first time. They are surreal, cinematic, poetic, and have real punch—with everything I could want in a collection of short fiction. Set in California and Europe, from the 1960s to the 1980s, they vividly capture lost times and lost places. They have echoes of Jack Kerouac and Paul Bowles, and can be read again and again with a sense of wonder and pleasure."—Jonah Raskin, Author of *Beat Blues, San Francisco, 1955*

"The effect of Meloan's lean poetic prose is raw, at times explosive, but often subtle in a way that is simply, cool. As other people burrow further down the digital portal of memes and fluff that repeat like meaningless fractals, instead grab yourself a copy of this book, and let it be your companion on your next train ride, layover, road trip, or trip into yourself…and good luck."— Westley Heine, Author of *Busking Blues: Recollection of a Chicago Street Musician & Squatter and 12 Chicago Cabbies*

"Meloan carefully crafts slices of life—of times and spaces—that take you to those places as if you just rolled up in the family station wagon or pulled into the station on a train. From descriptions of his family's arrival in the neon night of Los Angeles, to impossibly intimate exchanges with an East German border guard across the Berlin Wall, Meloan's writing is inspiring in its depth and sensitivity."—Steven Deeble, Author of *Persistence of Vision*

"These stories work like narrative prisms, simultaneously providing glimpses into the characters, the eras, and the places. The simple yet direct prose style draws you like a tractor beam into specific but vastly different corners of a multifaceted zeitgeist. They will stay with you, call back to you, days and even weeks after reading them."—Andrew O. Dugas, Author of *Sleepwalking in Paradise*

"Meloan's collection of stories is quintessentially Californian. Tales of his family's move to Los Angeles from Indiana chronicle a young boy's awakening to a strange collective dream inside the impact zone of the LA suburbs, the rapidly changing landscape of the West, and the behind-closed-doors affairs of those caught between generations and imprisoned by convention. His stories are a journey through a uniquely late 20th century experience, meticulously paced, and populated with complex, often outrageous people who drift in and out of each scene. His writing alternates between lively character studies and post-Beat prose poetry that leads the reader, as it must, from the midwest to San Francisco. *St. James Infirmary* is a joy to read." —Lisa Summers, Author of *The Green Tara*

"Meloan's collection of contemporary noir is for those who love adventures in the dark. The flashlight of his work throws a column of brilliant California sun onto the uncanny underground of everyday life." —AJ Petersen; Poet, Former Adjunct Professor at University of Iowa

"Steven's stories draw me right into his experiences, as if I am sitting next to him and hearing/witnessing the events in real time. With sharp insight and dry humor, he always takes a turn I don't expect. He writes with a haunting subtleness that lingers long after the story is told." —Carol Allison, Author of *The Sound of a Held Breath*

MORE ROADSIDE PRESS TITLES:

By Plane, Train or Coincidence
Michele McDannold

Prying
Jack Micheline, Charles Bukowski and Catfish McDaris

Wolf Whistles Behind the Dumpster
Dan Provost

Busking Blues: Recollections of a Chicago Street Musician and Squatter
Westley Heine

Unknowable Things
Kerry Trautman

How to Play House
Heather Dorn

Kiss the Heathens
Ryan Quinn Flanagan

Made in the USA
Middletown, DE
24 October 2023

41342575R00057